The Nurgla's Magic Tear

HARRY SECOMBE

Illustrated by Priscilla Lamont

PUFFIN BOOKS

PUFFIN BOOKS

Published by the Penguin Group
Penguin Books Ltd, 27 Wrights Lane, London W8 5TZ, England
Penguin Books USA Inc., 375 Hudson Street, New York, New York 10014, USA
Penguin Books Australia Ltd, Ringwood, Victoria, Australia
Penguin Books Canada Ltd, 10 Alcorn Avenue, Toronto, Ontario, Canada M4V 3B2
Penguin Books (NZ) Ltd, 182–190 Wairau Road, Auckland 10, New Zealand

Penguin Books Ltd, Registered Offices: Harmondsworth, Middlesex, England

First published by Robson Books Ltd 1991
Published in Puffin Books 1993
1 3 5 7 9 10 8 6 4 2

Typeset by DatIX International Limited, Bungay, Suffolk
Filmset in Monophoto Baskerville
Printed in England by Clays Ltd, St Ives plc

Katy looked out of her bedroom window and heaved a great big sigh. 'Oh dear,' she said to herself. She talked to herself quite a lot.

It was early evening and the sun was still visible above the trees at the bottom of the garden. Katy could hear the muffled sounds of voices coming from the party which her parents were having downstairs.

In her hand, Katy held a pale, tear-shaped pebble which she had found on the beach the moment after her friend Fred the Nurgla had disappeared.

She had met Fred on the island of Majorca when she had holidayed there with her parents out of season. Fred, a huge and fearsome-looking sea monster, had been basking in a deserted cove when Katy arrived and changed his destiny. Instead of being afraid of the Nurgla – who had terrorized mankind for centuries – Katy had befriended him. She had shared her picnics with him, read him stories and played house on the beach with him until it was time for her to leave for home. The tear that the Nurgla had shed at their parting held a significance that even Katy could not fully comprehend.

Unbeknown to Katy, her friendship with Fred had been closely monitored in a cigar-shaped space capsule by the Shining Ones – highly intelligent coloured blobs that communicated by thought. The Nurgla was one of these beings but, due to certain unforgivable incidents that he had instigated on Earth, he had been prevented from returning to the spaceship until he had been paid for an honest day's work, felt the touch of a human hand in affection, learnt to love and be loved in return, and, finally, had shed a genuine tear.

Fred the Nurgla owed his eventual reunion with his fellow beings to the little girl who now held in her hand his tear that had turned to stone as it had fallen down his ghastly green cheek and sizzled into the sea.

Katy's meeting with the Nurgla had taken place a year ago, and yet Katy still longed to see her old friend and playmate once more. Gently she rubbed the pebble between her fingers and shed a little tear for the Nurgla. It rolled down her cheek and splashed on to the stone in her hand. 'I do wish I could see you again, Fred,' she said softly.

Turning back to the window she rested her chin on the sill and gazed into the distance. As she looked she became aware of what at first sight appeared to be a hot-air balloon heading towards the house. However, it seemed to be going too

8

fast for one of those, and was nothing like as large. Suddenly, before she could work out what it was, a coloured ball of light about the size of a football hovered in the air right outside her bedroom window. It made no sound but just went round and round, glowing with a lovely red colour. Katy backed away from the open window, her hand still clutching the pebble. She was not afraid, but she was cautious of this strange object.

She examined it from a safe distance. Its colour began to change as she watched, going from red to dark blue and then to green, and suddenly it seemed as if it was all the colours of the rainbow all at once.

Katy was fascinated and took a step nearer the window. Then a voice in her head said, 'Katy, I came because you called me.'

It was a voice she had never heard before and yet somehow she knew it. It was sweet and yet strong, not loud but beautifully musical, and though she had never heard him speak she became aware with a rush of recognition which filled her mind and almost burst her heart that it was her Fred.

'Where are you?' she whispered.

'I'm here, outside the window. I'm the ball of light you're looking at,' said the voice in her head with a tinkle of laughter.

'But, but, what happened to your body?' Katy was bewildered. 'I want to give you a big hug and I can't very well do that to a – a coloured blob.'

'All right,' said the voice. 'I'll be

10

Fred again for you. But I'll have to make myself smaller or I shan't fit into your room.'

And in a flash, the Nurgla made his appearance on her bed. He was about the size of Katy's friend Emily's little Yorkshire terrier, but much the same Fred whom Katy had last seen on the beach in Majorca – except with a kindlier, more friendly face.

How's that?' he said with a flourish.

Katy stood absolutely still for a moment or two – something which her mother was always telling her to do but which she never did, unlike now. Then, with a cry of joy, she threw herself on to the bed alongside the Nurgla.

'Tell me where you've been. And why were you a coloured ball? And – and . . . ?'

The Nurgla blew twin clouds of smoke out of his nostrils. 'One question at a time,' said his voice in her head with a chuckle.

Briefly he told Katy that her kindness to him had saved him from being doomed to remain a monster for ever, and how when he went back to his own planet he was made very welcome and forgiven for all his misdeeds on Earth.

'But how did you manage to come back?' asked Katy. 'Your planet must be a long, long way off.'

'We can travel millions of miles in the twinkling of an eye,' said the Nurgla rather proudly. 'But in your case, the tear that I shed for you, which became the pebble you're holding in your hand, is very special. You see, when your tear splashed on it, it became a beacon sending out a signal so powerful that it could not be ignored. I happened to be in a spaceship circling Earth when your message came, and my leader, the Supreme Brightness, said that I must obey the cry from a little girl's heart because it's the strongest force in the whole universe. So here I am.'

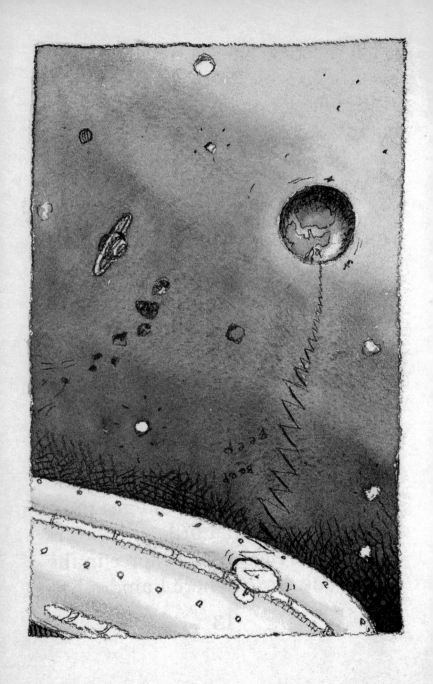

'How long can you stay? And please stop that smoking 'cos Mummy doesn't allow it in the house.' Katy waved a hand in front of the Nurgla's nose, trying to make the smoke disappear.

'I can only stay for two hours, I'm afraid. That is, two hours of *your* time, which is four gloxies in *our* time. I have work to do. You earthlings have made a nasty big hole in the ozone layer above your planet, and we've been sent to try and patch it up.'

Katy coughed as more smoke came from the Nurgla's nostrils. 'You're helping to make it bigger,' she said.

'My smoke is ozone-friendly,' said the Nurgla with just a touch of crossness.

Katy gave him a big hug. 'I'm so sorry,' she said. 'I don't want to quarrel with you when you've only just arrived.'

Just then there was a knock on her bedroom door. 'Who are you talking to in there, Katy?' It was her mother's voice.

Katy sat up quickly. 'It's Fred the Nurgla,' she called. 'He's come to see me.'

'Oh dear, not that again,' said her mother wearily from outside the door. 'She's had this obsession about a monster she's supposed to have met in Majorca last year,' she whispered to someone who was with her.

'My little girl had a phase like that too,' said her companion.

They moved on down the stairs. 'Can you smell smoke? I've threatened my husband that if he smokes that filthy pipe in my house

16

. . .' The voice faded away.

Katy looked at the Nurgla and shrugged her shoulders. 'I don't think Mummy and Daddy believe that you really exist.'

'Is that so?' said the Nurgla's voice in her head, thoughtfully. 'I think we can have some fun tonight. I really do.'

Downstairs the cocktail party was in full swing. About thirty of Katy's parents' friends filled the front room and dining room, and some of them had overflowed into the garden. Her father weaved his way in and out of the chattering guests, handing out drinks from a tray, while her mother supervised the buffet which had been laid out in the kitchen.

'Do have some more trifle, or perhaps another sausage roll,' she said to nobody in particular. It was difficult to hear what she was saying anyway, because the record-player was blaring out Beatles music.

Katy stood at the top of the stairs and looked down into the hallway. At her side, on the end of a lead made from one of her hair ribbons,

sat the Nurgla, who had suggested the idea.

'What a noisy lot of people,' said his voice in her head. He was still the size of a Yorkshire terrier but of course looked like a monster. 'Come on,' he said. 'Let's go and get something to eat.'

They started down the stairs, picking their way through couples who were sitting there eating off paper plates. No one took any notice of them at all as they progressed towards the kitchen. Her mother was leaning against the sink, sipping a glass of wine as she spoke to her next-door neighbour, Mrs Bramley.

'Nobody seems to be eating the sausage rolls,' she said.

'Pardon?' said Mrs Bramley. 'This music is awfully loud.'

'I said nobody seems to be eating the sausage rolls.'

As she spoke these words, the Nurgla's head came up from under the table. He extended his neck to twice its size and in a split second devoured two huge plates full of sausage rolls. His head then disappeared back under the table.

Mrs Bramley gave a little shriek. 'Did you see that?' she said to Katy's mother, who had turned her head away and missed what had gone on.

'Did I see what?'

'That – that awful thing that ate the sausage rolls.'

'Take more water with it, dear.' Katy's mother gave a little laugh and turned to speak to Katy: 'Don't make a nuisance of yourself now.' Then off she went into the other room remarking, 'Oh good, the sausage rolls have all gone,' as she passed the table.

Katy looked down to where the Nurgla sat blowing little puffs of smoke from his nostrils. 'I enjoyed that,' he said to her.

'How did you do that thing with your neck?' she asked as they moved off into a quiet part of the garden through the french windows.

'I can make myself bigger or smaller or give myself a longer neck or a bigger tail or anything I want to. But because this is how you last saw me, I have to be a sea monster. Of course on my *own* planet I can be anything I care to be.'

A large gentleman came towards them across the grass carrying an empty whisky glass. 'I say, little girl,' he said. 'Where does your daddy keep the whisky?'

Before Katy could reply the man gave a little jump in the air. 'Ouch! Your dog's bitten my ankle.'

'He's not a dog, he's a monster,' said Katy indignantly.

'I'll give him monster,' said the large man, aiming a kick at the Nurgla.

The next thing he knew he was

looking into a fearsome face with blazing eyes and flaring nostrils. The face lingered for a few seconds and then faded.

Katy looked at the large man. His eyes were like huge round saucers and his face was all black from the Nurgla's smoke.

'That's a big dog,' he said quietly to himself. 'That's the biggest dog

I've ever seen. That must be the biggest dog in the whole world.' He turned away and staggered off. As he went they heard him say, 'I think I'll go and have a lie-down in the lily pond.'

Katy knelt down beside the Nurgla and gave him a little hug. 'That was very naughty,' she said, giggling.

'I haven't had so much fun since I was the Loch Ness Monster,' Fred's voice chuckled in her head.

'Katy! Where are you?' Her father's voice came across from the house.

'I think you'd better stay out here for a while,' Katy said to the Nurgla. 'I'll go and see what Daddy wants. And try to keep out of trouble.' She ran off towards the french windows.

Fred watched her go. 'I could do with a good stretch,' he said to himself and, taking a quick look around to see that nobody was watching, he blew himself up to his full size. He now towered above the roof of the house and found that he could see into the bedrooms. Inside one of them he noticed Katy's mother talking to Mrs Bramley, the lady who had seen him taking the sausage rolls. He bent his head closer to the half-open window to listen to what they were saying.

'Perhaps you should lie down on the bed for a while,' said Katy's mother.

Mrs Bramley nodded. 'I've been over-working lately. Fancy thinking I saw a monster eating sausage rolls.' She laughed a little nervously and

lowered herself on to the bed.

Fred felt a bit sorry that he had frightened the lady and thought perhaps he should make amends. Putting his head through the window he tried to give Mrs Bramley a reassuring smile.

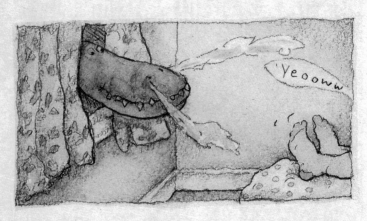

Katy's mother, who was busy covering her nervous neighbour with the eiderdown, making brisk little comforting noises, had her back to the window and so didn't see the ghastly sight of the Nurgla's attempt at a smile.

As he drew back his lips all his terrible teeth came into view and smoke trailed briefly from his nostrils.

Mrs Bramley, who saw it all, gave one tiny cry and passed out cold.

The Nurgla's head disappeared at once.

Katy's mother clucked her tongue. 'The woman's a nervous wreck. She needs a good holiday.' She sniffed the air. 'He's smoking that pipe again,' she muttered and left the bedroom to look for her husband.

'It's time you were in bed, young lady,' Katy's father was saying to her as her mother turned up.

'You've been smoking that pipe of yours again, the smell is all over the house, and that Mrs Bramley is having a nervous breakdown,' she said, without pausing for breath. 'And why aren't you in bed?'

'Who, me?' said her husband.

'No, Katy, of course. Come along.' She took Katy by the hand and moved with her towards the stairs.

'But Fred the Nurgla's out in the garden,' protested Katy. 'And he's got to go home soon. He's only got about two gloxies left. He's helping me mend the hole in the ozone layer.'

'What a vivid imagination you've got,' said her mother, marching her through the guests and up the stairs.

30

'I suppose that little toy dog you were dragging around on a piece of string is your monster.'

'He's not a toy dog and its not a piece of string – it's a hair ribbon, so there.' Katy's lower lip began to tremble.

'All right then, he's not a toy dog,' said her mother, trying to be kind.

'I'll ask Daddy to go and bring him up to you.' She opened the door and motioned Katy inside her room. 'Now go to bed, there's a good girl. Nighty-night.'

Down in a secluded part of the garden, near the gate, two figures were cuddling. It was getting dark now and Mary Postlethwaite and Nigel Blunkett were taking advantage of the fact. They worked in Katy's father's office and were extremely fond of each other. Katy thought they were a bit 'touched'.

From the benefit of his high viewing point the Nurgla could see them very clearly. He was intrigued by their goings-on and bent his head down to hear. Curiosity was his

worst failing. The perfume that Mary was wearing appealed to him. Tentatively he moved forward. He made no sound because if he didn't want to, he didn't. His forked tongue flicked out and touched the back of Mary's neck.

'Ooh!' she said. 'That tickles!'

'What tickles?' Nigel was surprised, because both his arms were firmly around Mary's waist.

The Nurgla took another taste of the girl's scent.

'Stop it, Nigel,' she giggled.

Nigel, who had his eyes closed, now opened them and found himself staring straight into the Nurgla's face. 'Aaaargh!' he said, removing his arms from Mary's waist. 'It's a – a – thingy!' He pointed over her shoulder, his eyes popping out of his head. Then he said 'Aargh!' again, and in one bound he cleared the garden gate and fled up the road uttering little whoops of terror as he went.

Behind Mary, the Nurgla had reverted to his little-dog size again.

'Whatever's come over Nigel?' said Mary in amazement, and then she turned and saw the little Nurgla.

'Fancy being frightened of a little thing like that. What sort of a man does he call himself?' She stamped her foot and, tossing her head, went back to the house.

Katy's father met her as she came in. 'Did you see a little toy animal out there in the garden?' he asked.

'Yes, it's down by the garden gate.

It just frightened the life out of
Nigel, the coward.'

The Nurgla kept absolutely still
as Katy's father approached. He
allowed himself to be picked up and
examined in the half-light. 'Funny-
looking thing. Wonder who gave this
to Katy?' her father said. 'Better
take it up to her. She gets very upset
when she loses one of her toys.'

He knocked on Katy's door. 'I've

got your little monster thing here,' he called.

Katy opened the door. 'Where is he? Has he caused any trouble?' She was relieved to see Fred in her father's hands.

'Caused any trouble?' Her father chuckled. 'No, he's behaved himself very well.' He handed the Nurgla over and went off down the stairs shaking his head in disbelief, 'That's a good one – caused any trouble, indeed.'

Back in Katy's bedroom the Nurgla shook himself and settled down on the bed. 'You humans are very jumpy, you know,' said his voice in Katy's head.

'What do you mean?' asked Katy sharply.

'Oh, nothing.' The Nurgla didn't

want to go into any explanations. Katy might not have approved of his behaviour in the garden. 'What are you doing?' he asked to change the subject.

Katy was standing by her little dressing-table looking at some exercise books. 'I've just remembered I haven't done my homework and it's got to be in tomorrow morning. And you have to go back to your spaceship soon. Oh dear.' She was close to tears.

'Don't cry,' said the Nurgla gently, because he loved her dearly and didn't like to see her upset. 'What do you have to do?'

'It's history,' said Katy. 'I have to write about Britain in the Stone Age and I'm not very good at it, and . . . and . . .' Tears began to well up in her eyes.

'Perhaps I can help you. I can move backwards and forwards in time.'

'Yes, but we've only got about an hour left before you have to go. That's two thingummies in your time.'

'Two gloxies,' said the Nurgla. 'We can go back to the Stone Age in a split second.'

'How can I come with you?' asked Katy, dabbing at her eyes with a tissue.

'Just hold the tear I shed for you in your hand and sit on my back.' As he said the words the Nurgla grew to the size of a small pony.

'Be careful with your tail,' cautioned Katy as she got astride his back. 'You nearly knocked my china cat off the dressing-table.'

'Before we go, have you got a watch? Because where we're going clocks haven't yet been invented and I must not be late getting back,' said the Nurgla.

'I'm wearing the wrist-watch Daddy gave me for my birthday,' said Katy proudly.

'Good. Now close your eyes.'

Behind her closed lids Katy was aware of a sudden flash of colour and then came a great rush of wind. She kept her eyes shut, afraid to open them.

'We're here,' said the Nurgla's voice.

Slowly Katy opened her eyes. They were on a vast plain with

rolling tree-covered hills blue in the distance. The sun was shining and little puffs of cloud floated dreamily across the sky.

'Ooh! It's lovely!' Katy clapped her hands in delight, dropping the tear as she did so.

'Be careful with the tear, because without it we can't get back. I mean *I* can, but *you* can't.' The Nurgla's voice was very firm.

Katy got off his back and picked up the little stone tear, putting it in the pocket of her jeans. She jumped up and down on the grass with excitement. 'Where shall we go? What shall we do?'

'Well, you have a walk about and I'm going to have a little doze before I go back. This earthly sunshine makes me sleepy.' The Nurgla yawned. 'But don't worry, the "tear" will look after you. If you get frightened by an animal or something, just hold it in your hand and wish to be made bigger and you'll grow as tall as you wish. But don't forget to say "*Scroop*" or you'll keep growing.'

'*Scroop*?' said Katy. 'What kind of a word is that?'

'It's a magic word from our planet.' The Nurgla's voice in her head sounded very sleepy. He gave another big yawn, and rolling over on his side, he closed his eyes. 'Don't forget the time,' he said and fell asleep.

Katy looked at him a little worriedly. She thought that at the very least he would have given her a guided tour of the place. 'Oh, never mind,' she said to herself. 'I shall just have to go for a walk on my own.' Katy was a very resourceful little girl and was never too worried about things.

She looked around her, wondering which way to go. Then, in the distance, about a half a mile away, she saw a little collection of conical huts. 'I'll go and ask the people who live there what it's like to live in the Stone Age, and then I can go back and do my homework.'

She set off towards the huts, enjoying the warmth of the sunshine and the scent of the flowers and the grass. Strange birds she had never seen before flew overhead making harsh cries.

As she approached the huts, several dogs came out and started

barking a warning. From the nearest hut an unkempt figure, covered in dark hair and wearing the skin of some animal which Katy could not recognize, lurched into view. He was carrying in one hand a sort of axe which had a bone handle and a head made of stone. At the sight of Katy he dropped his axe and stared

in amazement. He gave a succession of calls in a strange guttural tongue and more people emerged from the other huts. The men all wore skins and carried weapons and the women among them also wore clothing made from animal hides. Some hugged babies to their bosoms, and children of varying ages clung to their legs. One little girl of about three started to run towards Katy, curious to see this stranger at closer range. A woman, obviously her mother, ran after her and dragged her back to the enclosure.

Two of the dogs, getting bolder now, began to approach Katy, making soft growling noises in their throats.

'Oh dear,' thought Katy, reaching for the tear in her pocket. 'Perhaps

I'd better get a bit bigger.'

The dogs were within leaping distance of her and were a fearsome sight with wolf-like fangs and yellow eyes, the hair raised in ridges along their backs.

Katy held the tear firmly in her hand and wished to be made bigger. Immediately she began to grow and in no time was at a level with the tops of the huts.

The dogs squealed in fright and dashed back to the compound and the rest of the community disappeared into their various homes uttering cries of sheer terror.

'That's big enough,' thought Katy, and tried to think of the word the Nurgla had told her to use to stop growing. '*Floop!*' she said, but she kept on upwards. '*Sloop!* . . .

48

Groop!' . . . still she got bigger. Then she remembered. '*Scroop!*' she cried – and she stopped growing.

'Thank heavens for that.' She breathed a sigh of relief and looked down. She couldn't believe her eyes. The huts looked like the little straw umbrellas which her mother liked to put in the drinks when they had visitors. 'I must be about twelve metres tall,' she thought, putting the tear back in the pocket of her jeans.

She knelt down and tried to look into one of the huts, but the entrance was too small for her to see anything. Then she decided there was only one way to find out what was inside, and very gently she put her thumb and forefinger around the pole sticking out of the top of the hut and carefully lifted off the roof. In the

middle of the floor a fire was burning
and at first the smoke obscured her
view. She waved her hand over the
topless hut to remove the smoke and
became aware of a little group of
people clinging to each other and
making frightened cries.

'I'm not going to hurt you,' said
Katy, and at the sound of her voice
the little people clapped their hands

to their ears. 'I only wanted to know what life is like here in the Stone Age, but I don't suppose you'd be able to understand what I say anyway.' She looked carefully around the contents of the hut and made a mental note of them.

Taking care not to damage it, Katy placed the roof back on. She stood up and wondered what to do next. Fifteen minutes had gone by on her watch so she had another forty-five minutes to go before she and the Nurgla had to return.

It was fun being a giant, thought Katy. She could see for miles, and when she started to walk away from the huts, she found that even the bigger animals were quite small in comparison to her size. A deer with huge antlers crossed her path and

stopped, petrified with fear at the sight of this huge figure. Katy stooped and picked it up, smoothing the silky hide and trying to soothe its pounding heart. 'I wish I could tell him that I only want to be friends,' she thought as she placed the deer back on the ground, where it bounded away without a backward glance.

She came to a river where lines of

rafts made of logs were drawn up alongside both banks. As soon as she appeared, the group of men who were unloading them took one look at her and ran away in all directions, their screams tiny in her ears. Katy bent down to examine what the men had been taking from the rafts. They were stones, all of them shaped like the dominoes that she had been given for Christmas by Mrs Bramley next door. She picked them up and piled them on the shore. They had a bluish tinge and Katy was fascinated by them. She decided to play 'house' with them and, taking them some way from the river to a nice flat piece of grass, she began to place them in a circle. Then she laid some of the stones across the top of the circle. When she'd had enough, she

went back to the river to wash, first taking off her wrist-watch. She looked around after she had swilled her hands and face for something to dry herself with. The grass wasn't long enough and then she remembered the handkerchief in her jeans' pocket. She pulled it out and as she did so the tear dropped to the ground without her noticing. It fell among some of the blue stones on the river bank and because it had grown along with Katy it was about the same size as them.

All the activity and excitement had made her feel tired and so Katy stretched out on the ground. Her wrist-watch lay alongside her and looking at it she noted that there were twenty-five minutes left before she had to go back. 'I'll just lie here for a couple of minutes and then I'll go and find the Nurgla.' Katy closed her eyes, just to rest them, and promptly fell asleep.

Meanwhile, about ten metres away, the leader of the men who had been unloading the barges lay on his stomach in the grass observing the sleeping Katy. He was very brave, but his heart was bumping loudly. Very loudly. So loudly that after a time he realized that what he could hear was not his heart. The sound was coming from where the giant lay.

The man's name was Ug, son of Ag, and he was a chief. He and his men had brought the stones on the rafts, travelling many miles in the process, on the instructions of Bo the Peep, who was a priest. They were to be used to build some kind of temple. Ug wasn't quite sure what, and he was very annoyed that this huge giant had come from nowhere and taken them away. He realized that there was not much he could do about it, but he was afraid of what Bo the Peep would say when he

found out that the stones had been
stolen. He might be turned into
stone himself by the priest, who
could be rather nasty.

He wondered what he could do, all
the time aware of the loud thumping
noise coming from near the giant.
Raising himself on his elbows, he
could see that Katy was asleep,
and spotting the wrist-watch he
realized that it was that monstrous

thing which was making all the noise.

Suddenly an idea came to him. If he could somehow get the strange noise-maker away from the sleeping giant, Bo the Peep might not be so angry about losing the stones. Squinting his eyes against the sun, Ug studied the object. It had two enormous black animal-skin ropes either side of a thick round device which reflected the light of the sun, and from inside this came the mysterious, magical thumping sound.

Behind him he could hear his men returning fearfully to see what was happening. He turned to them and told them of his plan to take the magic object from the giant to replace the stones they had lost. The men shook their heads, saying it was too dangerous. But after Ug had pointed out that Bo the Peep could have them all turned into stone, they reluctantly agreed to do what he said.

Cautiously they crept forward and Ug issued instructions in a low voice as to how they would drag it away between them. Ten men would surround the head of the giant armed with spears in case it awoke, while the others would carry the magic device away down to the river. 'It's got to be done quickly,' he whispered, having a little trouble doing so owing to the bone he wore through his nose. And so, as the watch ticked away, the fearful Stone Age men removed it from where it lay near Katy's head and loaded it on to one of the log rafts. Only ten minutes had passed on the watch

face, which wasn't bad for the first jewellery theft in history.

Katy woke with a start, just as the raft disappeared around the bend.

'What's the time?' she asked herself in a panic. She looked to where she had left her wrist-watch and saw that it had gone. She looked in the pockets of her jeans, thinking that perhaps she had put it in one of them and then she found that the tear had gone too. Now, Katy was a pretty level-headed little girl under normal circumstances, but these circumstances were hardly normal.

She stamped her foot down hard, causing a derelict hut in the enclosure a mile away to collapse. 'Fred the Nurgla, where are you?' she cried, sending thousands of birds wheeling into the sky. Down-river, the men on the log raft with its loudly ticking burden shivered at

the sound of her voice and paddled faster.

It seemed ages before Katy heard the Nurgla's voice in her head.

'I'm coming,' it said and suddenly he was there at her ankle. 'Oh,' he said. 'I'll come up to you,' and he became her size. 'What's the matter?'

Katy told him between sobs that

not only had she lost her watch, but the tear had gone too.

The Nurgla was worried. 'I should have come with you and this would not have happened,' he said. 'I was having a little chat with Ptom the Pterodactyl – he's doing a monitoring job for our planet.'

'What are we going to do?' said Katy, blowing her nose.

'The first thing is to find out how many gloxies we've got left,' said the Nurgla reflectively.

'How can we do that?'

'There is a way of telling the time on our planet in an emergency – let me see, now . . . how do we do it?'

'Oh, come on, please – do hurry up.'

'I think I've got it,' said the Nurgla, putting his tail in his mouth

and going a peculiar shade of purple. Slowly, along his side, large green figures appeared. 'What does it say?' The Nurgla's voice was tight with strain.

'I can't read what it says,' said Katy desperately.

'Oh, I'm sorry. I'll translate it into English.' His voice was apologetic. He repeated the process, this time going a delicate pink colour.

'It says, "You have three minutes to go." Oh dear, I'll never get home now.' Katy began to cry big tears.

The Nurgla watched her with pity in his eyes. Then he said, 'Quick, come and cry over here by these stones, if one of *your* tears lands on *my* tear it will glow a deep red.'

'I don't think I've got any tears left.' Katy was heaving dry sobs now.

The figures on the Nurgla's side read: 'You have two minutes to go.'

'Take your hanky out of your pocket.'

'It's soaking wet,' said Katy.

'I know. Wring out your tears over this pile of stones and let's see what happens.'

Katy fumbled for her handkerchief

and came over to where the Nurgla stood. His side now read: 'You have one minute to go.'

She squeezed her handkerchief as hard as she could, showering the stones with shed tears.

'That's it! There!' cried the Nurgla's voice. 'Quick – it's under that stone over there.'

Katy seized it with a cry of happiness and held it tightly.

'You have thirty seconds to go,' read the Nurgla's side.

'Jump on my back quickly,' called the voice in Katy's head.

She sat astride his back and shut her eyes tightly. There was a flash of red and the same great rush of wind, and when Katy opened her eyes she was back in her bedroom, her proper size.

'Oh! Thank you, thank you,' she cried, hugging the Nurgla.

'I must go, my dear,' he said gently. 'I've only about ten of your seconds to get back to my spaceship.' He dissolved into a ball of brilliant green light. It came close to Katy and she felt it caress her face for an instant.

'When you want me really badly I'll come to you. And tell your friends to take care of this planet Earth. If you don't you haven't many gloxies left. Goodbye.'

And Katy watched the glowing ball fly through her window and out into the night sky. She stood watching it become just a tiny spot of light and then vanish. 'I shall miss you so much,' she said quietly, and taking the tear from her pocket, she kissed it and put it away carefully in the drawer of her dressing-table.

Back in the Stone Age, Ug arrived at Bo the Peep's hut, dragging the

magical device he had found on a sled made of logs. Before he could say anything Bo shook him warmly by the right ear – that was how the tribe showed gratitude. 'You've done a good job on that temple. How did you manage to do it in such a short time?'

Ug looked puzzled.

'Look – over there,' said Bo, turning Ug around and pointing to the grassy plateau behind the village. On it stood a perfect circle of

giant stones with other stones placed across the top. 'Well done. I think I'll call it Stonehenge. You shall have another bone to wear through your nose. Now, what have you got here?'

Bo examined the strange object from all angles. 'It's too magical for everybody to see. We must dig a hole and hide it. It will be the deepest hole in the world.' Bo was warming to his theme. 'And then we'll build a great hill on top of it. Come, let's start digging.'

And Ug, who didn't really fancy another bone through his nose, picked up his piece of antler horn and, with a deep sigh, started to dig.

Katy's mother came into the sitting-room and sat down heavily in her favourite chair. 'I've just been next door to give Mrs Bramley a bowl of beef tea. She thought she saw a flying saucer last night. Poor woman's going potty.' She picked up her knitting.

'Have you read this?' Katy's father looked up from his paper.

His wife stared at him. 'No,' she said. 'You have the paper.'

'Well, it says here that archaeologists excavating around Silbury Hill have come across what appears to be an enormous wrist-watch. Fancy that – a Stone Age wrist-watch.' He shook his head in disbelief.

'That must be mine,' said Katy excitedly. She was looking at the top marks her history teacher had

72

given her for her Stone Age essay. 'I
lost it in the Stone Age.'

'Don't be silly, Katy,' said her
mother with a little sniff.

Katy heaved a big sigh and sat
back in her chair. 'They'd never
believe me, anyway,' she thought to
herself. Then she put her hand in
her pocket and gently massaged the
tear pebble. 'But we know it really
happened, don't we, Fred?' she

whispered. And she felt something like a tiny puff of air caress her cheek, and she smiled a little secret smile.

OLGA
Takes Charge

Michael Bond

**Graham was in love. There was no
doubt about it.**

Olga da Polga cannot believe that her
friend Graham the tortoise has fallen for
someone who doesn't speak and who is so
tall that he cannot even see her eyes.
With her usual sense of 'sorting things
out', Olga sets out to discover what's
really going on in the garden.

Also in Young Puffin

MAGIC IN THE AIR

Phyllis Arkle

People miss a lot, not believing in magic.

Sam believes in magic, and he's the only person in the town who sees Weathervane Witch fly off on her magic broomstick. It doesn't take Sam long to find out why: thieves have come to steal wild birds' eggs, and the four precious eggs in Golden Eagle's nest are in danger. But with Sam and Weathervane Dragon's help, Weathervane Witch is determined to foil the robbers!

Adventures of ZOT the DOG

Ivan Jones

Life is fun with Zot!

Zot is a lovable little dog, and he and his friend Clive have all sorts of funny adventures. There's the cheeky mouse who plays tricks on them, a cunning snake who steals all the food, and an unhappy frog who does NOT like being swallowed up by Zot the dog!

Also in Young Puffin

THE LITTLE WITCH

Margaret Mahy

Some stories are true, and some aren't...

Six surprising tales about sailors and pirates, witches and witch-babies, orphans and children, and even lions and dragons!